BUT!

by Tim Hamilton

Holiday House / New York

I was going to dedicate this to pirates everywhere,
BUT . . . I should probably dedicate it to my mother and
father, who always made sure my head was warm.

Copyright © 2014 by Tim Hamilton
HOLIDAY HOUSE is registered in the U.S. Patent and Trademark Office.
Printed and Bound in April 2014 at Toppan Leefung, DongGuan City, China.
The artwork was created with pen and ink, watercolors, and digital tools.
www.holidayhouse.com
First Edition
1 3 5 7 9 10 8 6 4 2

Library of Congress Cataloging-in-Publication Data
Hamilton, Tim, author, illustrator.
But! / by Tim Hamilton. — First edition.
pages cm
Summary: In Halibut Bay, Eddie and his dog Phil must give up their plans for fishing
to help ailing Aunt Sue with her chores, which include throwing a pirate birthday party for Sue's friend, Captain Rugbeard.
ISBN 978-0-8234-3046-8 (hardcover)
[1. Chores—Fiction. 2. Parties—Fiction. 3. Birthdays—Fiction. 4. Pirates—Fiction.
5. Hats—Fiction. 6. Dogs—Fiction.] I. Title.
PZ7.H1826588But 2014
[E]—dc23
2013021127

Eddie lived with his dad and their dog, Phil,
in Halibut Bay, where hats were hard to come
by and people had cold heads.

On this particular Friday, Eddie and Phil
looked forward to a fun weekend of fishing,
BUT...

Eddie's father stopped them in their tracks.

"Your aunt Sue tripped on some yarn and broke her leg while making a pair of polka-dot socks!" he said, while rubbing his cold head. "You have to do her chores."

"No fishing?" Eddie cried.
"No fishing?" Phil cried.
"No fishing," Dad said.

"Watch for pirates!" Dad shouted as Eddie and Phil sailed off. "And keep your heads warm," he added.

Eddie and Phil had a good headwind and encountered no pirates,

BUT...

they were still very late!
  "Hurry!" Aunt Sue shouted.
"I've been waiting with this
cold head of mine!

"Here's your list of chores.
They all need to be done today,
BUT...

"you must do them quietly!
I need to sleep, and I'll be very,
VERY angry if you wake me!"
And with that she sent
them away.

Eddie and Phil swept, washed dishes, and did laundry.

"Oh no!" Phil shouted as he looked at the list of chores. "Did you see this? We have to throw a party today! And not just any party,

BUT...

"a pirate birthday party for Aunt Sue's friend
Captain Rugbeard! It says we need to get him
a good present or he'll be furious."

"A pirate birthday party?" Eddie said. "I've never
been to a pirate birthday party. What do we need?"

"Same as any birthday party," Phil said.
"Cake, ice cream, and at least one balloon."

So they made a cake and thought about what
to give Captain Rugbeard for a present. They came up
with all sorts of good ideas, like a treasure chest
filled with gold doubloons and
pieces of eight,
BUT...

the only things they could find in the house were
socks that Aunt Sue had made. And Phil and Eddie
didn't think those socks were the kind a pirate would like!

"Normally, I'd say get him something
else," Phil said,

"BUT...

"we have no choice! The pirates are here!!"

"Surprise!" Eddie and Phil shouted when the pirates got to the door.
Everything was ready,

BUT...

Eddie's heart sank when he saw that Captain Rugbeard had only one leg, because Eddie and Phil were giving him two socks!

"ARRRG!" Captain Rugbeard shouted. "Even though my head is cold, this is a great party! I can't wait to open my presents,

BUT...

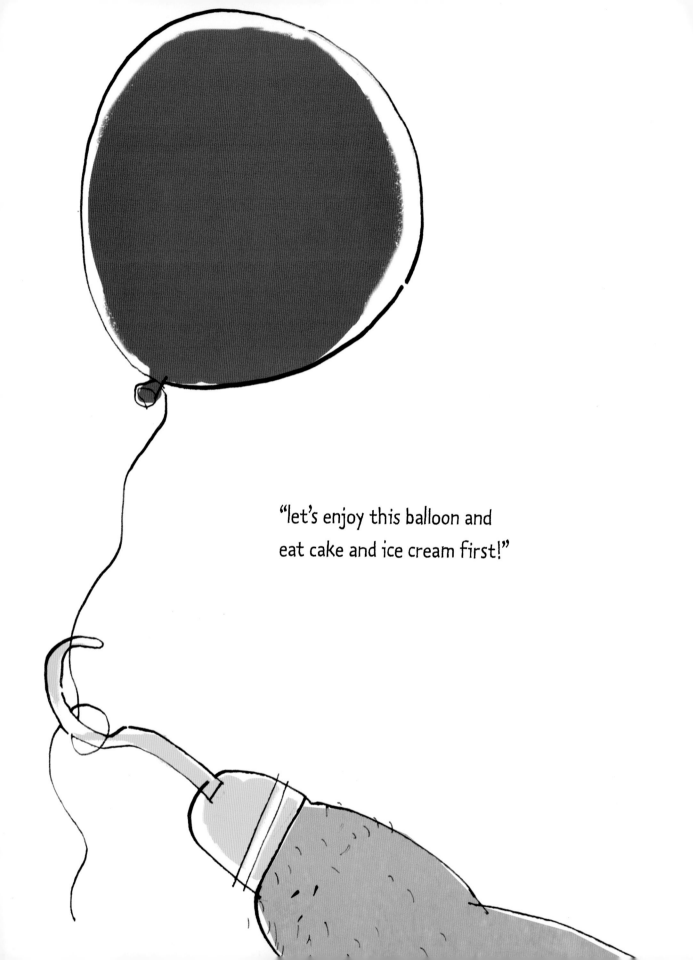

"let's enjoy this balloon and eat cake and ice cream first!"

As the pirates gave Rugbeard his presents, Eddie
was horrified to see what they were: termite repellent,
wood polish—all presents for Rugbeard's wooden leg!
Eventually, Rugbeard wanted Eddie's present,

BUT...

Eddie had hidden it.
"I don't know where
it is," Eddie said. "I must
have lost it!"

Eddie was feeling hopeful,

BUT...

a smelly pirate named Stinky Joe found
the present behind a chair.

"Arrrg! How nicely wrapped," Rugbeard
said. "I'd hate to tear this lovely paper."
BUT...

he did. Rugbeard looked confused.

"What are these?" he asked. "They look like a pair of socks!"

Rugbeard was about to get VERY, VERY angry,

BUT...

just then a cold breeze blew through
the window, giving Eddie's head a chill
and his brain an idea.

"They look like socks," Eddie said,

"BUT...

"they are actually a matching **hat-and-sock set!**"
Captain Rugbeard mumbled and grumbled as
he tried on the hat and sock.

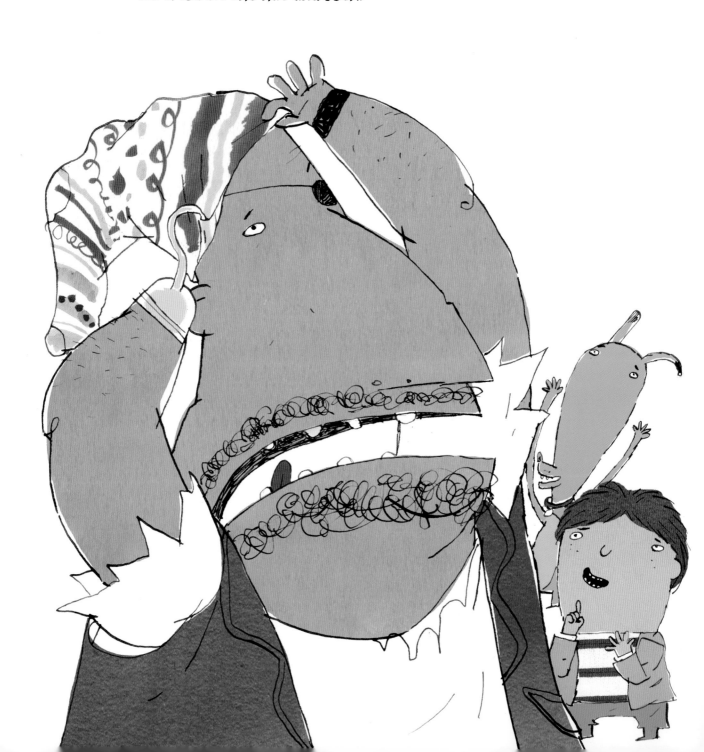

"ARRRG!" he shouted! "My head is warm—**YO-HO-HO!**"
And so things seemed to be okay,

BUT...

Captain Rugbeard's shouts woke
Aunt Sue; and true to her word,
she was VERY, VERY angry until . . .

the other pirates wanted matching hat-and-sock sets and
gave Aunt Sue many gold doubloons and pieces of eight.
You may think that is the end of the story,

BUT...

everyone in Halibut Bay heard about Aunt Sue's matching hat-and-sock sets. So now all the citizens of Halibut Bay have warm heads,

BUT...

everyone has one cold foot.